Bobby Normal
And The
Virtuous Man

A.S.Chambers

First published by Basilisk Books in 2021
This edition published in 2024.
Copyright © 2024 Basilisk Books.

A.S.Chambers asserts his moral right to be identified as the author of this work.

Cover art © 2021 Liam Shaw.

ISBN: 978-1-915679-49-9

DEDICATION

For Susan and all those
little fluffy cuddles you gave me.

ALSO BY A.S.CHAMBERS:

Sam Spallucci Series.
The Casebook of Sam Spallucci - 2012
Sam Spallucci: Ghosts From The Past - 2014
Sam Spallucci: Shadows of Lancaster – 2016
Sam Spallucci: The Case of The Belligerent Bard - 2016
Sam Spallucci: Dark Justice – 2018
Sam Spallucci: Troubled Souls - 2020
Sam Spallucci: Bloodline – Due 2021
Sam Spallucci: Fury of the Fallen - Due 2022

Short Story Anthologies.
Oh Taste And See – 2014
All Things Dark And Dangerous – 2015
Let All Mortal Flesh – 2016
Mourning Has Broken – 2018
Hide Not Thou Thy Face - 2020
If Ye Loathe Me – Due 2022

Ebook short stories.
High Moon - 2013
Girls Just Wanna Have Fun – 2013
Needs Must - 2019

Novellas.
Songbird – 2019

Bobby Normal Series.
Bobby Normal and the Eternal Talisman - 2021
Bobby Normal and the Children of Cain - Due 2022

Omnibuses.
Children of Cain - 2019

ACKNOWLEDGEMENTS

A huge thank you to Ashleigh Hunter and Jack Knight for their excellent proofreading skills.
Plus many, many thanks to the incredibly talented Liam Shaw for once more putting up with my incredibly vague ideas and producing yet another magnificent cover.

CONTENTS

Previously...

Bobby was a teenage boy from Irlingbury. He lived there with his eight-year-old sister Katy. Like most people in the Divergent Lands, they existed in a life of abject poverty. Many years ago, a being called Kanor rose like a black dragon over the entire world and decimated the human race by use of his creatures forged from clay, the constructs.

To make matters worse, the children's father had been executed for treason, leaving them to fend for themselves in this inhospitable land. Not only this, but they were frequently singled out and tormented by an older boy by the name of Teller whose family were allowed privileges as the bully's father was a quisling of Kanor's regime. This made Teller feel superior and, looking down on Bobby with derision, he labelled him "Normal".

Bobby and Katy met a girl named Persephone whose father was dying. She asked them to deliver a wooden token called the Eternal Talisman to someone called the Man of Virtue in the neighbouring village of Orchester. She claimed that it would aid him in destroying the vile Kanor, thus liberating their world. On their journey they were harried and subsequently captured by Teller and his gang of cronies before being liberated by a strange shape-shifting old man who called himself Cutter.

Upon reaching Orchester, they were tracked down once again by the vengeful Teller who abducted Katy and threatened to kill her. The small girl fought back and pushed him to his death over the side of a bridge, an action for which she showed no apparent remorse.

We rejoin them on their adventures just after they reach the house of the Virtuous Man…

Chapter One

Bobby was nervous.

He realised that this seemed to be a perpetual state of affairs at the moment. As he and his eight-year-old kid sister Katy entered the small ramshackle house in the village of Orchester, he thought back to a few days ago, to what now seemed like a different lifetime. They had been living as street urchins in the unimportant, mostly forgotten village of Irlingbury, a settlement like so many in the ravaged Divergent Lands of the mysterious dark overlord, Kanor. The two of them had been impoverished orphans, living off scraps they could scavenge or food they could steal. It had been a hard life, but it had also been a simple one. They had known what to expect, be it a swift kick from an irate trader or a hurried escape through the derelict streets of a dying village.

There had been no drama, so to speak. The worst that they could have expected was the unwanted attention of the obnoxious bully Teller, a boy a few years older than Bobby, and his doting little band of cronies.

But now, as of a short while ago, Teller was dead.

Katy had killed him, pushed him over the crumbling side of the bridge in the main street of Orchester.

And she had shown no remorse. None whatsoever.

Bobby's stomach knotted double then triple as he recalled Katy simply standing, peering over the side of the broken bridge at the distorted body of the boy she had just killed. He couldn't just let this matter slide. He was going to have to talk to her at some point.

But not right now.

Now they had to tend to the matter that had dragged them out of their simple routine of sleep, steal, run, eat.

Pushing his hand into the pocket of his ragged, dirty trousers, he wrapped his fingers around a small, hard object. His thumb traced a pattern that had been meticulously carved into the wood: a cup and a blade. This was the Eternal Talisman. Back in Irlingbury, he and Katy had encountered the girl named Persephone and she had entrusted them to take the talisman to the next village, Orchester, where they were to deliver it to an individual named Jason, the Virtuous Man.

He was going to use it to kill Kanor.

Bobby's stomach rolled again. Kanor was the being who had brought about the Divergence, who had used his constructs, his animated clay golems, to reduce the human race to a mere remnant. Known as the black dragon, no one had ever seen his face. Well, no one had seen his face *and lived*. And this small piece of engraved wood was supposed to help destroy him.

Bobby sighed.

He wanted to go back to his simple life. This was just not for him.

He wasn't a hero, someone who went on quests to slay unseen monsters.

He was *normal.*

The teenage boy thought about how Teller had labelled him with the moniker as an insult, saying that he was a nobody, no one special. But now he realised that normality was something that he desperately wanted back in his life. They would hand the Eternal Talisman over and go, return to Irlingbury and forget that this had ever happened.

But there were questions, weren't there?

Before he had died, Teller had said something about Bobby's and Katy's father, who had been executed by Shadow Wraiths when Katy was just an infant. He had said that Howard had been a traitor, that he had been plotting against Kanor. A part of Bobby wanted, no *needed,* to know more about this. Perhaps this Virtuous Man would have some answers?

"Are you okay, sonny?"

Bobby snapped out of his deep reverie and looked up at the elderly woman who had greeted them on the doorstep, a look of concern touching her grey eyes. "I'm okay, thank you. Just tired."

She nodded. "I imagine so. I'm guessing you've had a long journey."

"Not particularly," he shrugged, "just eventful." *And that is a true understatement,* he thought to himself.

"Well," she smiled benevolently, warmly rubbing his shoulder, "why don't you come on through and meet Jason. While you're doing that, I'll rustle up some food."

Bobby nodded, swallowed his nerves and accompanied her through to the back of the house, Katy following on his heels.

They emerged into a small room. The windows were tightly shuttered, allowing neither light nor inquisitive eyes to penetrate from the outside. It was illuminated by a collection of candles that were dotted around in the corners and by a roaring fire that burnt furiously in the ancient stone hearth. There were two old chairs positioned facing the fire. Bobby recognised them as wingbacks. He recalled his father Howard, who had been a skilled carpenter, manufacturing such items of furniture, taking great care in shaping the precious pieces of wood into ornate sides that allowed the head to rest at an angle when the sitter had dozed off.

The man that was seated in the wingback on the right was far from asleep. He was sat staring intently into the flickering tendrils of flame that were dancing in the fireplace. The waltzing red glow illuminated his face as he smoked slowly on the long pipe that was clasped between his lips. His hair was long and dark. Along with an accompanying beard, it framed a pair of eyes that were currently not in this room; they were staring off into and through the fire to somewhere far and distant.

Bobby had a feeling that he did not wish to know what those eyes were looking at.

"Jason," the elderly woman whispered as the logs in the fireplace crackled and spat. "It has arrived."

For a moment there was no movement from the quiet, bearded man. Then his head rose just a fraction, as if his mind was processing what it had been told, before he turned, looked at the children and nodded. "That is good." His speech was simple, plainly stated. "Please," he gestured to the other chair, "join me." Then to the woman, "Thank you, Joyce. Could you please let the others know?"

The woman nodded, smiled at Bobby, then left him and Katy with this curious man.

Bobby looked down at Katy. The eight-year-old looked fit to drop. "Go on," he said. "I'm okay."

She climbed up into the chair, curled up and promptly fell asleep.

"The little one must be exhausted," Jason observed, taking another draw from his pipe. "Have you come far?"

"Only from Irlingbury," Bobby explained. "But..." His words just drifted off, not wanting to recall the journey again.

The man's dark eyes held him, exploring what he had just said, then nodded. "I see."

There was an awkward silence as the two remained there a moment, just watching each other over the popping and hissing of the fire. Bobby thought that he was a strange individual, not what he had expected. But then, what *had* he expected? Some sort of brash warrior, clad in shining armour? Or perhaps a well-spoken general, a leader of troops? He wasn't sure, but he knew that it hadn't been this odd man who hardly spoke. He sighed, dug his hand into his pocket and pulled out the Eternal Talisman. "I believe that you need this?"

As Bobby passed the small wooden token over, he saw, for the first time, a change in the man's expression. Excitement filled his eyes and the corners of his mouth turned up underneath his ragged beard. He began to shake his head as if it was hard to believe what he was actually holding and then small tears edged their way out of his eyes. He turned to Bobby, gripped the boy's arm in a firm hand and whispered breathlessly, "Thank you. Thank you so very much."

"That's okay," Bobby shrugged, trying to feign a certain amount of casualness, "Like I said, we didn't exactly have to travel far."

The Virtuous Man settled back into his

wingback chair. "But, that is not so. Sometimes, what seems like the smallest of feats can have enormous repercussions. The fate of the world can often hang upon the action of one man, or," he pointed to Bobby with his pipe, "one boy. So never underestimate anything that you do. All is connected." He turned the mouthpiece of the long pipe back around to his lips and took a long draw before blowing fragrant smoke up into the air.

Bobby tried not to cough. His father had not been a smoker. Howard had seen it as a frivolous, pointless and noxious act of self-indulgence. "It weakens the lungs and dulls the senses," he had stated bluntly one day when they had been watching local women gathering herbs for drying. "Imagine all that smoke going down into your body. It isn't good for you. Would you stick your head in a fireplace and gobble up woodsmoke as if it were a broth? Of course not. Mind you, it used to be worse." He had paused, sighed and continued. "People used to smoke something called tobacco. They knew it was dreadfully bad for them; it coated their lungs with tar and killed thousands. Yet, still they did it. Just like people accept their lives as they are now: drudgery, pointlessness and enslavement. It is all they can remember, so it is all they will accept.

"Somebody needs to change it."

A small cough escaped through Bobby's contorted lips and the smoker smiled. "I see you are not a fan. I have to admit, it is the one small vice that I have. I find it helps me think. It clears my mind." He paused, then continued. "Tell me, lad, what is your name?"

"Bobby."

"And the young one?"

"She is my sister, Katy."

"I was told that a girl named Persephone was supposed to be bringing me the Talisman. Where is she?"

"She received news that her father was gravely ill. She had to return to see him before he died and we volunteered to bring the Talisman the final length of its journey."

The man took another draw from his pipe and nodded. "I see." He held the Eternal Talisman in his hand, his thumb running over the carved engraving of the cup and the knife. "My family is dead, as I am guessing is yours?"

Bobby nodded.

"Death, Bobby, is a natural part of existence. With life, it forges a duality that balances all the universe. We cannot have one without the other. If everyone lived, life would be misery because there would be no space, no food. If everyone died, then life would again be awful as our species would be extinct within a generation. This is something that Kanor knows and uses well. He keeps humanity just at the brink of death, breathing in the occasional spark of life to rekindle us and sustain us in a weakened state to use us as tools in the field or as hunting practice for his minions of clay. Death, as life, is to be expected. It must be accepted and endured so that we can forge onwards for the greater good.

"Sacrifices must be expected."

Bobby frowned. "Are you saying that Persephone should have ignored the news of her father and carried on with her mission?"

"What is the life of one man compared

to the life of the world? Persephone knew of that when she agreed to bring me the Talisman." He sighed. "They should have entrusted it to someone older."

Bobby felt something burn deep down in his gut. Back in Irlingbury, Persephone had saved Katy and him from Teller. She had helped them escape. The older girl had been incredibly torn with regard to her duty and returning to her ailing father. For this man who had never met her to sit here and criticise her… It felt incredibly unfair. Bobby opened his mouth to say something, when he heard Katy stir in her armchair. "Is it dinner time yet?" she yawned.

Chapter Two

Bobby thought that Katy's eyes were literally going to pop out of their sockets when they sat down to eat. Her mouth hung open and, for once, she was devoid of all comments as she surveyed the feast that had been lain out in the dining room of the small house. He had to admit that his stomach was also enjoying the sight and smell of the home-cooked food. It was expressing its anticipation by roaring louder than a stampede of horses.

"I take it you're hungry, then?" Joyce chuckled as she finished setting the table.

Bobby settled himself down. "Definitely. I can't remember when we last had a meal like this. It must have been when our father was still alive. We've really had to scavenge for scraps since then."

"Bless your souls!" the woman exclaimed. "How long ago has he been dead?"

Bobby shrugged. "I've sort of lost count. Katy was still a babe."

Joyce intently studied the features of his face. "You're from Irlingbury, you say?"

The boy nodded.

"Was your father a carpenter? Howard?"

Bobby started. "You knew him?"

Joyce smiled sadly. "Indeed, I did. You look just like him, you do." She paused, as if there was more that she wanted to say. "I… I was saddened to hear what happened to him, with the Shadow Wraiths. We all were. He was a good man."

Bobby opened his mouth. Did this kind woman know more about his father? Could she shed light on Teller's revelation that he had been some sort of covert conspirator against Kanor? However, at that moment, Jason entered the room, followed by six people, all adults. Bobby studied the newcomers as they came and seated themselves at the large table. They seemed well acquainted with each other, talking quietly amongst themselves, so he supposed that they were residents of Orchester. Their clothing was simple, homemade; the attire of village folk. Four were men; two were women. As they seated themselves, the villagers gave quick, inquisitive glances towards the two strange children. One of the two women sat next to them and greeted them with a friendly smile. The other woman sat on the opposite side of the long table, next to one of the men. She gave his hand a quick, affectionate squeeze as she settled herself down. Bobby guessed that they were a couple. One of the men sported a wild shock of ginger hair. He seated himself down at the far end of the table, where he fiddled constantly with the tips of his fingers as he kept glancing up towards Jason then over to Bobby and Katy. The woman who had seated herself next to Bobby reached across and gently squeezed his forearm, offering him a reassuring smile. The final two, slightly younger than the rest, sat together just between Jason and Katy. Bobby noted the similarity in hair colour and facial structure. He guessed that these two were brothers. In all, the group looked just like any other collection of people that one would encounter in the street: some were related, some not; some took matters in their stride, others worried over the minutiae of details. They certainly did not look like a group of people who were intent on overthrowing the dark power that had enslaved their world.

But then, neither had his dad. Perhaps looks could be deceptive?

Jason took the head of the table. He seated himself down, waited until everyone else had settled themselves and spoke quietly, "Friends. Today is a momentous day. As I am sure you have noticed, we have been joined by two new young friends: Bobby and Katy."

The six villagers gave greetings to the children before Jason continued.

"But, more on that later. First, we dine and discuss matters of the day. Please, bow your heads."

Bobby frowned and glanced at Katy. His sister just shrugged back as perplexed as he was, so they both lowered their heads as asked, keeping one eye on Jason.

"Father," Jason continued. "We thank you for this bounty of food on our table and for the hands that have crafted and cooked it. We thank you for the arrival of our guests and your wonderful gift that they have brought to us. We praise your holy name. Amen."

The six others and Joyce replied, "Amen," and began to help themselves. Katy didn't need to be asked twice and dived in herself, piling her plate high.

The woman who had smiled at them as she had sat down laughed. "It would appear that your sister has an appetite larger than her stature."

Bobby shrugged. "Tell me about it. She's constantly hungry."

"I guess she is growing."

"I guess." Bobby helped himself to what he recognised as chicken and some sort of green vegetable whose identity was a mystery. "I'm Bobby and my sister is Katy."

"Pleased to meet you, Bobby. May our hearth be warm for you. I am Rose. Have you travelled far?"

"Just from Irlingbury," he managed around a mouthful of roast fowl. "Can I ask something?"

Rose nodded.

"Who was Jason talking to just then? Before the meal."

The woman lifted an eyebrow in curiosity. "You've never heard anyone say Grace before?"

Bobby shook his head.

"Jason is a priest. You know what one of those is?"

"Sorry, but I don't."

"Well, a priest is a man or a woman who serves God and ministers to His people here on Earth. The priest guides them and teaches them the words that God's son taught us thousands of years ago, before wicked men put him to death."

Bobby chewed his food thoughtfully. "Why was he killed? God's son, that is."

"Because he spoke the truth that the rulers of his time did not want to hear," came Jason's solemn voice from the head of the table. He sat, his dark eyes framed by his hair and beard. "It was a very, very long time ago. His name was Jesus. He lived in a distant land, far away from here, across the sea, across another continent."

Bobby became aware that everyone, even his sister, had stopped eating and all attention was now focussed on Jason.

"He spent his life tending to the sick and giving people hope that, one day, the tyrannical rule of man would be overthrown and that God would enter people's hearts, illuminating them with His love and bringing peace to the world."

"But why would the rulers want him dead?" Bobby asked. "Surely what he was teaching was a *good* thing?"

Jason gave a small, rueful laugh. "Not to those who control their people in a hand of fear. Those wicked men had their subjects exactly where they wanted them. Whatever they said was law and that kept them in power, making them incredibly wealthy. The common populace was no better than slaves as the power of the rulers spread out over the face of the known Earth. They demanded taxes and tribute to strengthen their armies and expand their greedy empire. Their subjects either gave willingly or were put to the sword as an example. There could be no opposition. Dissent was quickly and brutally quashed. They would take those who spoke against them and nail them to crosses of wood, leaving them to die an excruciating death before their withered bodies were devoured by carrion birds.

"Such was what happened to Jesus."

"So, he failed?"

"So the rulers thought. So they thought. But, three days later, a miraculous thing transpired. He rose from the dead and appeared to those who were closest to him. He instructed them to go out into the world and spread his message of peace and love, to minister to the poor and the protect those who were powerless."

"But he hasn't stopped Kanor, has he?"

A hush fell across the table at Bobby's words.

"For all his words, the Divergence still came and Kanor rose. I don't see anyone rising from the dead to stop him."

Some of the diners muttered amongst

themselves, annoyed with what they saw as the impertinence of the boy. Jason lifted a hand and they fell silent again. "What Bobby says is true. The words of our saviour did not prevent the rise of Kanor. We cannot deny that. When the black dragon emerged, the world was unprepared, at peace. It is even said that angels had walked amongst us."

"Was this after the Battle?" one of the two brothers asked.

Jason nodded. "Yes, the great Battle on the plains of Megiddo, when the angels defeated the army of constructs."

"Wondrous day," the woman opposite whispered.

"Wondrous day," her husband echoed.

Bobby frowned. This was all far too complicated for him. They were talking about things of which he had never heard and certainly did not understand. "You're saying that an army beat a whole bunch of constructs? I've seen one up close, when I was younger. Those things are indestructible."

A smile touched Jason's lips. "Not at all. In fact, that is why I have summoned you all here tonight. We're going hunting."

The plan, according to Jason, was simple. Actually, it was so simple, that the creations of Kanor would never expect it. As the diners continued to eat, he spoke about how the constructs did, in truth, have a weakness; their physical make-up. "As we know, they are made from clay. Kanor drew them up from the very ground itself by the use of some arcane magic which breathed life into their inanimate bodies. So it is, that when people have tried to attack the golems in the past, what has happened?"

"Their weapons plunge into the abominations' bodies with no effect," answered the man on the opposite side of the table.

"Even if you cut off their head, the creature will just grow another," said his wife. "It is the same for any of their limbs. They are indestructible."

Jason popped some bread into his mouth and chewed it in a thoughtful manner before picking up the plate upon which it had been sat. "Clay, is a most useful material, is it not? It can be hewn inexpensively from the riverside and moulded or shaped to whatever the potter or craftsperson desires. Look at this plate for example. It is a simple, utilitarian device that is intended for us to eat our food from. It is made from the same substance as those creatures out there that stalk the land and destroy our families, is it not?"

There were tentative nods from around the dining table.

"Yet, it is decidedly different in its physical properties." He knocked a knuckle against the plate's surface, creating a dull thunking noise. "Why is that?"

"It has been fired," Bobby said. "My father took me to a potter once, when I was little. We needed a new water jug. I watched the potter take a tray of identical jugs that he had made from soft clay and place them in an incredibly hot oven. They baked and became hard. I was fascinated."

Jason smiled his appreciation. "Very good, young one. And did you acquire a jug on your shopping trip that day?"

Bobby nodded, remembering the day well, walking home with his father, being allowed to carry the bright red jug in his small hands. "Yes, we did. My father let me carry it home. It was the most beautiful thing: a vivid scarlet, and its glaze shone brightly in the sun."

"Ah! And I guess your father gave you a very special piece of advice as you carried that jug. A warning, perhaps?"

Bobby chuckled. "Oh, he certainly did. He told me not to drop it."

There was an almighty crash as the plate tumbled from Jason's hand and smashed to pieces on the hard floor.

"Constructs," he growled, "are no different to the pottery that we make on a daily basis. In their current state, they are soft, pliable and able to be repaired. However, if we fire them, we can break them!

"For too long now, we have cowered in our houses, in our hovels, terrified at the creatures that stalk the highways and byways of our land. *Our* land, not *theirs*. We have considered them to be super-human, unstoppable. Yet, they are no different to the very plates off which we eat, to the cups from which we drink. I have received word

that, in a few days' time, a party of three constructs is due to pass by this village. We are
going to lure them into a trap, bake them
solid and grind them into dust. We will show
the people of this land that the time has
come for us to rise up against our oppressor
and throw off the shackles into which he
bound us, enslaved us. If we destroy his
army, then he will be defenceless and I will
be able to walk into his lair unhindered and
do what needs to be done."

Jason paused, took a moment to com-
pose himself and continued. "This brings me
onto the most joyous news and the reason
why we have to strike now. As you know, I
am tasked with the mission of slaying the
vile Kanor, that black dragon, which is why I
have journeyed here from my own home, a
home that was ravaged by his soulless monsters. Well, the last few days have proven to
be most auspicious. Just yesterday, I was
walking in the old cemetery on the outskirts
of the village, taking in the air and searching
my soul for answers. I wanted to know how
I was supposed to defeat a monster like
Kanor. As I wandered, I saw a crypt that

stood out from the others. It was incredibly plain, but upon its lintel was an emblem that struck me as unusual. It was of a cup and a knife."

Bobby's ears pricked up at the reference to the same image that was upon the Eternal Talisman.

"As you know, there has long been whisperings of two things known only as Eternals: one a Cup, one a Blade. Things older than time itself which Kanor craves for some mysterious reason but, as yet, has been unable to find. So, I was drawn to enter this tomb and inside I found, under a loose slab of stone, a box. Inside, was this." In a swift movement, he drew a long knife out from under his cloak and lay it reverently on the table. It was bright silver in colour and its blade was wavy in shape. There were gasps of amazement from the rest of the diners. Jason just nodded. "I know. I have told you before of the stories I have heard that there is one weapon that can kill Kanor: the Eternal Dagger. It was forged centuries ago by a very wise, holy man who knew that, one day, the man of virtue would rise to take arms against the Black Dragon. It was imbued with the grace of God himself, giving the Virtuous Man, me, the ability to end this Divergent Land in which we live."

The table sat in awed silence until Katy swallowed her current mouthful of food and said, "It's incredibly shiny. It looks like new, not old."

Bobby felt the atmosphere in the room become somewhat awkward as all eyes turned to his outspoken kid sister.

"I had a little spoon once," the girl continued, oblivious to the attention. "Daddy gave it to me. It was made from metal, so he said it was very precious. It was so shiny that I could see my face in it. That was because it was brand new. I can see my face in that shiny knife too. Also, it's a funny-looking shape. You couldn't cut anything with it. Ow!" She turned and glared at Bobby, who had just kicked her under the table.

A deep chuckle came from the head of the table. "From the mouths of babes," Jason smiled. "See how the child recognises the pureness of this dagger, how it is so different to any other mortal weapon. This is why it will destroy Kanor when I plunge it deep into his cancerous heart."

"But how will you be able to reach him?" asked the woman sat next to Bobby. "His lair is surrounded by the lake that he created in the middle of Wellington."

Jason reached out and lay the Eternal Talisman on the table. "Because, thanks to our young guests here, I now have this. The Eternal Talisman will bring me safe passage across the lake. All I have to do is to present it to the ferryman, and he will carry me across.

"As you can see, God has not deserted us. He has provided us with the means to destroy this evil for good. All we need to do now is to stack the odds in our favour by thinning Kanor's vile army."

Chapter Three

The next few days were a flurry of activity. Jason decided that the best place to confront the constructs would be in the old cemetery where he had found the Eternal Dagger. "It is out of town, so we will not run the risk of others being wounded or killed by Kanor's creatures. Plus, it is a rabbit warren of old tumbledown buildings, which will serve our purpose well."

The plan, he explained, was simple enough. They were to cause a commotion as the three constructs approached the village and then lure them, unsuspecting, into the cemetery. "They are mindless beasts, so they will undoubtedly follow, their main directive being to kill all those who cause trouble." Once they had the constructs' attention, they were to get the pursuers to chase them through the cemetery and into the old chapel.

Bobby stood and frowned at the derelict building. The roof was long gone, destroyed by wind and rain, and the timber from which the walls were fashioned looked frail and brittle. "It doesn't look capable of holding one construct, let alone three," he said.

Jason smiled. "Ah, well that's all part of the plan. The beasts will see it the same way that you do and will blithely charge in. Once in, there will be no escape. We will spend today ensuring that every hole in the walls is filled in and packed tight with timber to make sure that it is escape-proof. After that, we will gather dry timber from what wood we can scavenge in the locale. We will pack it into every corner of the chapel as more fuel for the fire, along with the dry wood from its walls."

"But surely it is too large a space to trap them in? Three constructs do not take up much room. They'll be able to move freely and avoid any fire."

The Virtuous Man chuckled. "That is

where our final surprise will come into play. After they have charged blindly into the chapel, we will make sure that they have congregated into its narrowest part, the sanctuary." He pointed to the far end of the old building. "You see how it is a fraction of the width of the rest of the building? Well, we will take what is left of these old pews and make a wall to barricade them in. It will be hefty enough to prevent them from escaping. Then, when they are secured in that tight space, we shall rain fire down upon them and they shall bake."

Bobby frowned. "But how can we be sure that they will enter the sanctuary? What is to stop them from just turning around and heading back out?"

Jason pointed out a small hole at the base of the wall behind the ruined high altar. "You see that space up there? Well, someone will have acted as bait and will have lured them in on a fruitless chase. Then, when the constructs are close enough to almost catch their prey, that individual will duck down and bolt out of that hole to safety before the wall of pews is thrown into position."

"But, that hole is tiny. Who do you think would fit through it?"

Bobby's heart sank as Jason's eyes alighted on his sister, Katy.

"I really don't think this is a good idea."

Katy huffed and rolled her eyes as she carefully filled another clay pot with vegetable oil and placed it in a row with twelve others. "You just think I can't do it because I'm a girl."

"No. That's not it at all. I just think you can't do it because it's suicide." Bobby rolled his thirteenth fuse from a bundle of dried grass and inserted it into Katy's pot of oil. "The whole thing sounds crazy." He carefully cast his eyes around to make sure that they couldn't be overheard. The other villagers were either hard at work nailing old pews together to make a hefty looking barricade or were bulking out the walls of the sanctuary with kindling and straw, materials that would instantly ignite on impact from the fiery pots of oil that they intended to hurl in from above. "I just don't think that the constructs will buy it. Jason says that they are mind-less, but that's not my experience." The image of the construct in the village square at Irlingbury drifted into his mind. Its wet laugh still filled him with dread. "I'm worried that they will catch you."

Katy shrugged as she filled another pot ready for Bobby's fuse. "Not a chance of that. Teller couldn't hurt me, so neither will some heavy-footed clay monster."

Bobby watched his kid sister methodic-ally filling her pot with oil. What had happened to her on that bridge? She still showed no remorse in her killing of Teller. Last night he had watched her drift off to sleep. There had been no nightmares, no twitching or sleep talking. She had rested peacefully all night. Surely she should have been disturbed? This just didn't feel natural.

"How's it going?"

The children glanced up. It was Rose, who had sat next to them at the dinner table. Her hair was bound behind her head and her forehead was drenched with sweat. Her clothes were covered in wood shavings and splinters.

"I think our job is easier than yours," Bobby observed.

Rose's mouth turned up in an easy smile. "Ah, but it'll be worth it, won't it? Imagine what people will say when we destroy three of those creatures?" She knelt down next to Bobby and began to help him roll more fuses for the makeshift incendiary devices. "It will be the dawn of a new day."

"You really think so?"

"Of course. Jason has it all planned, doesn't he? He is the Man of Virtue. He will lead us to victory over Kanor."

Bobby's eyes fell on the bearded man as he wandered around the cemetery, watching over those who were going about their work on his master plan. The man nodded in approval at bundles of dry kindling, he smiled as he pulled at firmly constructed scaffolding that rose up behind the sanctuary. Bobby watched as Jason supervised and praised, yet didn't actually do any of the manual work himself.

And that worried him. It worried Bobby a great deal.

Chapter Four

Eventually, the day came. Bobby and the others had laboured incessantly at their preparations until Jason was satisfied with their work. The decaying walls of the church were now packed with timber and kindling. The makeshift barricade of ancient pews had been assembled and placed next to the sanctuary. Neat rows of incendiary pots were lined up along the near non-existent roof of the old church.

Jason nodded in satisfaction as he surveyed the work for the final time. He tugged at patched up holes, pushed against solid pews and peered into oil-filled pottery. "Excellent," he nodded. "Excellent, indeed. The constructs won't stand a chance."

The villagers smiled, albeit somewhat

wearily. They appreciated the thanks for their hard work.

"Do you all know what tasks you have?" he asked them.

They nodded and listed off their allotted roles. One group, the couple and the brothers, was to cause a disturbance to attract the constructs before darting into the shadows of the chapel, behind the makeshift barrier. Katy was to go along with this group and was to split off from the others, leading the constructs down the central aisle and up into the sanctuary. Once the barrier was in place, the second group, consisting of Bobby, Rose and the ginger-haired man, were to throw down the incendiary devices from the roof as Katy crawled through her small bolthole in the wall.

"A simple but effective plan," Jason smiled. "I am sure that, with God on your side, you will not fail."

Bobby frowned. "*We* will not fail? Will you not be fighting alongside us."

Jason gave a mocking laugh. "Bobby, someone has to let you know when the constructs are coming. That will be me. You see that ridge over there?" He pointed to a rise to the north of the cemetery. "I will lay in wait, watching the road for when they approach. When they do, I shall catch the light of the sun with the Eternal Dagger. It will glint three times to say that the enemy approaches. It is by far the most dangerous task of all. I will be on my own and at risk of being spotted by these creatures. I will need to time my signal precisely so that you know of their imminent arrival and so that they are not forewarned."

Bobby's frown refused to be parted from his forehead. It made sense, sort of, but there was something deep down that he did not like about this plan. Something he could not put his finger on.

He had a terrible feeling inside that it was all going to go wrong.

A while later and the sun was rising into the morning sky. Bobby had heaved himself up onto the roof of the church, taking his position on a makeshift scaffold that the villagers had constructed over the previous days. He grimaced as it creaked ominously under his weight.

"You doubting my handiwork?"

He looked up to see Rose grinning at him as she lifted a sackcloth off the pots that contained the highly flammable oil. It had been lain across them the night before to prevent dew settling on the wicks, rendering them damp and useless.

Bobby couldn't help but smile back. Over the last few days, he and Katy had spent more time with the amicable woman than any of the others. The rest of the villagers had been welcoming, but not over-friendly. It was as if they had too much on their mind, were too preoccupied with the task at hand to get to know the newcomers as well as they should. Rose had been different. She had chatted away to them quite happily, asking them about their life in Irlingbury, enquiring about their father, marvelling at their adventures on the way to deliver the Talisman. "I'm just not used to being this far off the ground," he said.

"You'll get used to it." Rose checked a fuse over and nodded in satisfaction. "Plus, it's not like we're going to be up here long."

"I suppose."

The woman eased herself into a seated position and her eyes studied the boy's face. "You seem somewhat unsure. What's the matter?"

"It's just... I don't know. I have my doubts about the plan."

"Really? It seems quite simple. We lure them in then bake them. Job done." She watched his eyes flick towards the small hole in the back of the sanctuary wall. "You're worried about Katy?"

"What if something goes wrong? What if the constructs catch her?"

"They won't. Bobby, look at me."

He lifted his eyes and gazed into her smiling face.

"Everything will be fine. You're not on your own now. Should anything... *untoward* happen, I've got your back. Okay?"

Bobby looked into those trusting, hopeful eyes for a moment, then nodded. "Okay," he finally agreed. "Okay."

The other villager on the scaffold patted Rose on the shoulder. "There's the signal: three flashes. It's time."

It all happened so quickly. One moment, they were stood atop the scaffold, waiting for the signal, the next...

The first thing of which Bobby was aware was a noise. It seemed to be coming from far off, but he knew that that wasn't really the case. He knew it had to be the other villagers catching the attention of the constructs. He listened carefully and could start to make out shouts and cries, before a raucous cheer drifted up to them from the road and was followed by the sound of running feet. Human feet.

The feet of the constructs made a very different sound altogether as they took up the chase.

Thud, thud. Thud, thud.

Precise and in time. Marching together in a slow, methodical beat. They pursued the humans, safe in the knowledge they were at no risk from the frail mortals. They would hunt them down, kill them, carry on with their journey. Unemotional. Unstoppable.

Thud, thud. Thud, thud.

"I can see them!"

Bobby followed Rose's gaze and spotted the party of villagers running as fast as they could, off the road and through the cemetery. He looked frantically for Katy, terrified that she would not be there, but swallowed his nerves as he saw her dart out in front of the pack towards the church.

And there, just entering the boundary of the old graveyard, came the three constructs.

Impassive. Relentless.

Thud, thud. Thud, thud.

The villagers down below reached the chapel and darted inside. Bobby carefully peered over the parapet as he watched the adults hide themselves behind the improvised barrier that had been made to appear as if it were just a pile of old wooden furniture. Katy, however, took centre stage in the middle of the ruined building. There was no look of fear about her person as she pulled back her shoulders and began to shout out all manner of things in order to keep the attention of the constructs, who had now reached the threshold of the building.

Bobby chewed on his bottom lip as he moved around to his station, readying himself to throw down the incendiary devices. As he eased himself around the scaffold, his eye line shifted and, for a moment, he caught sight of the road coming towards the cemetery. For the tiniest moment of time, he thought he caught sight of a figure on a horse riding towards them, but then he was pulled back to the here and now as the constructs bore down on his sister.

Katy played her role perfectly. She teased and taunted the clay creatures, all the time backing up towards the killing room of the sanctuary. She eased herself up against the back wall and continued to hurl abuse at them.

"She's good," Rose smiled at Bobby.

"She's practised lots on me," he replied.

The constructs followed, just as Jason had insisted they would. They took the steps up into the sanctuary.

Thud, thud.

They were no more than five arm lengths from the small girl.

Bobby felt as if his heart had stopped beating and his lungs were no longer drawing breath.

Then there was an almighty crash as the walls of the chapel shook when the barricade was forced into place. Bobby and the two villagers actually had to steady themselves against the decrepit wall of the church as their scaffolding swayed slightly. The constructs realised that something was amiss and turned to confront the wooden wall that had not been there just a moment before. One reached out and its arm transformed into a lance, piercing the wooden structure which shook precariously from the impact.

"Now!" the ginger-haired man shouted as he started to hurl his ignited pots down onto the constructs.

Rose did likewise, but Bobby halted as the pots struck, causing flames to rise up the walls of the sanctuary.

Katy was still down there! She was tugging frantically at a piece of timber that had slipped down the insides of the wall. The force of the barricade must have caused it to come loose. She was trapped in a burning room with three constructs!

"Katy!" Bobby yelled across the rising inferno, but she couldn't hear him. She just continually tugged in vain at the wedged timber.

The eyeless head of one of the constructs swung around and up towards the source of the shout then across to Bobby's sister, its thick tongue slithering across its lips as if scenting the air like a predatory serpent. There was the unmistakable sound of transformation and the boy screamed frantically as one of its clay arms snaked out and whipped itself around the small girl, dragging her across the rough floor.

"Katy!" Bobby screamed again. This could not be happening. It just couldn't! That monster had her! It was going to kill her. He watched in vain as Katy kicked and screamed against her assailant while the other two constructs continued to lance the barricade across the front of the sanctuary.

Then Bobby was aware of movement to his left as Rose vaulted over the side of the wall and clambered down the loose woodwork. At the last moment she leapt from the wall and launched herself into the construct that was holding Katy. Her impact caused it to lose its footing. It stumbled backwards, disoriented, and its grip on Katy slackened, allowing the girl to run towards the hole in the wall once more.

"Katy, go!" Rose screamed as the small girl tugged at the piece of now burning timber, prying the weakened wood from its hole and scampering out.

They were to be the woman's final words.

Bobby gaped in horror as he saw the prone construct reach out and plunge a lance into her back. Rose gazed down in confusion at the point sticking out through her chest before she fell limp, dead. The mindless golem paid her no more attention and rose, turned towards the barricade and joined its companions in battering at the wood.

The wood that was now aflame from the burning oil.

It was then that Bobby realised the major flaw in the plan that had been niggling away at him.

There was an almighty crash as the barricade gave way, its improvised structure weakened from the fire. It was like the logs over a fire pit when they have reached a critical point of burning; there is no more strength left in their crumbling structure and they just collapse.

The constructs strode through unimpeded, framed in a curtain of fire.

The four villagers let out a terrified shout and turned to flee, but they found their way blocked by a stranger dressed in black, his hair unnaturally smooth against his scalp. Bobby thought back to the lone horseman from before and his stomach lurched. It was a Shadow Wraith; the villagers were doomed.

The three constructs did not attack the panicked villagers, instead they worked their way around them, their arms outstretched, corralling them into one single spot, then the Wraith struck. He was so much more fleet of foot than the other creatures. A wicked smile spread across his face as he leapt from the floor, spun in the air and reached out with an arm that transformed into a sharp scythe-like blade. Bobby was aware of a wet cutting sound then watched in blood-chilling horror as the villagers' heads parted company from their necks and tumbled to the floor. Their bodies stood headless for a moment, as if in shock and unable to comprehend that they were now dead, lifeless, before they too fell to the floor of the chapel.

The Shadow Wraith withdrew its scythe back into a hand, flexed its fingers, then looked up at the wall where Bobby and the last remaining villager stood. It smiled once more and turned to walk out of the church, the three constructs following.

"We need to get out of here," the man whined, partly to Bobby, but mostly to himself as he ran his shaking fingers through his ginger curls. He snapped round and began to frantically clamber down the rickety scaffold. Bobby dragged his eyes away from the carnage in the burning church and followed suit. The improvised footholds and ladders swayed terribly under the weight of the two fleeing humans, but they made it down in one piece. Bobby turned to ask the man where they should go, but the villager was already running away, around the side of the church, back towards the village, towards the safety of his home. All Bobby could do was watch dumbfounded as he was left abandoned to fend for himself. Then, as the man passed out of sight, Bobby heard a dreadful scream and a sickening ripping sound. The fleeing man came back around the side of the church, impaled and writhing on the end of the Shadow Wraith's arm. His hands slapped helplessly at the clay lance and his legs kicked spasmodically as blood flowed out of his mouth, until he fell limp and lifeless off the simple but effective weapon.

The Shadow Wraith peered without emotion down at the dead human before flaring his nostrils, catching the scent of its next intended victim.

It looked across the churchyard, straight at Bobby.

Bobby froze. This was it. He was going to die. He had no hope. There was nothing he could do. He should just stand there and accept his fate. He would let his legs go weak and motionless. He would give himself to this superior creature.

The Wraith nodded and smiled as if it knew what the teenager was thinking, but then it frowned as a scream echoed across the churchyard.

It took Bobby a second to snap out of his reverie, to realise that the screaming human voice was aimed at him, but then the words seeped into his confusion, pulled away at the fabric of the clouds that were smothering his will to live and a familiar voice reached his ears.

"Bobby! Bobby! This way!"

At once, he was snapped back into his true senses and he saw Katy standing in the shadow of a grove of trees waving frantically, beckoning for him to follow her.

As the three constructs appeared round the corner of the burning church to join their superior, the boy, needing no further encouragement, rammed his legs into gear and shot after his kid sister.

Chapter Five

Don't trip! Don't trip!

These were the only words screaming through Bobby's head as he and Katy crashed and ripped their way through the undergrowth of the all-surrounding, claustrophobic woodland. To trip was to fall; to fall was to die. They had size and agility on their side. They could leap over fallen tree trunks and dive through narrow gaps which were too small for their pursuers. However, they were only human and eventually their muscles would tire and they would have to stop to rest and recuperate.

Constructs, being monsters fashioned from clay, did not have this problem.

They may have been slower, but they were relentless, unstoppable.

Bobby did not dare to glance over his shoulder for even a split second. To do so would be to take his concentration away from the task at hand — staying alive — yet he knew in grim detail what was behind him. It was the slow, methodical beat of heavy clay footsteps grinding down all that stood before them, confident that, in the end, they would catch and dispatch their quarry.

The outcome was inevitable.

Already, Bobby could feel his lungs starting to burn and his calves beginning to tremble as exhaustion began to take hold of his mortal frame. The constructs would know nothing of this. They were the ultimate killing machine.

And then there was Katy.

She was just eight, still in single fig-ures. What must she be feeling right now? Without looking, Bobby knew that she was right beside him. He could hear the snap-ping of twigs and the harsh, erratic gasping of her breath as she, like him, dodged and wove her away around the densely packed trees. Surely she couldn't sustain this frantic pace for much longer? She would stagger, trip, fall...

No! Don't think it! Don't give in! There had to be a way to escape. There had to!

"When you think that all is lost," their father had used to say when life was even harder than normal, "something will always present itself. You just need to keep your eyes and ears open, your senses alert, and be ready to follow the new path that life presents."

Hot tears of exertion streamed down Bobby's face as he recalled his late father's calm, philosophical voice. A path! What he would give for a path right now! In the last few days, his life had presented him with just problem after problem. They had ranged from a hoard of rats to a sociopathic bully; from a fanatical leader of an underground rebellion to questions about his father. Not to mention the worries about his kid sister that continually gnawed away inside of him.

But it had most certainly not provided so much as a simple path through a forest!

The branches and twigs whipped at his face, scratching him, causing his skin to sting. Reflexively, he lifted a hand to protect his eyes, obscuring his line of sight for just a split second...

And then the unthinkable happened. Bobby's hand fell away and he watched helplessly as the world around him slipped up over the horizontal. The ground came crashing up towards him as he instinctively stretched his hands out in front to soften the blow of the ground hurtling towards his face. His feet parted company with the treacherous woodland floor and he was aware that they were now higher than his head as he tumbled forward and landed in a heap on the ground.

Ground which was incredibly wet, sticky and stank abysmally.

Something will always present itself.

His eyes snatched around him, taking in his situation in an instant and he quickly called out to his sister, "Katy! Here! Quick!"

The small girl ran over and joined him then tried to protest as he rapidly began to cover her with the putrid filth from the stagnant pond. "It might just save us," he explained. "Quick! Cover yourself!"

And all the time, he was waiting for the

twofold beat of the relentless footsteps of their inhuman pursuers.

In less than a minute, the two children were covered from head to toe in black, foul-smelling filth. Bobby caught his sister's hand and dragged her down to a secluded point of the pond that was overshadowed by a fallen and decaying tree. Quietly, they edged their way down, out of sight.

Just in time.

Thud thud.

Thud thud.

Thud...

The heavy footsteps ground to a halt just on the other side of the tree trunk. The two children held each other tight as they shivered in the cold stagnant water. They clenched their teeth tight to prevent even the slightest noise of chattering. The slightest noise and they were dead.

"Well?" came a harsh, commanding voice. "Nothing?"

Bobby and Katy held their breath as the Shadow Wraith climbed up on top of the fallen tree to survey the surroundings. They were aware of the creaking of the damp wood above them as the creature turned around, trying to locate them with its eyes that they knew were blacker than night. Bobby kept his arm tight around his sibling and they remained motionless, petrified.

Never before had they been so scared.

Eventually, the Wraith leapt off and landed heavily on the ground behind them. "We've lost them," it said and the distinct sound of the constructs marching off through the woodland resumed.

Bobby and Katy waited.

They waited some more.

They continued to wait.

When they could bear it no more, they crawled out from under the tree and emerged into the forest. They eased themselves upright to see the light of day above them and were confronted by the grinning face of the Shadow Wraith who was sat nonchalantly against a tree by the side of the pool.

"Patience truly is a marvellous thing," he grinned as he rose gracefully to his feet, his limbs languid and supple, clearly not made from flesh and blood or bound by the mortal constraints of hard, rigid bones. The children didn't have a chance to run as his arms snaked out beyond any humanly possible length and grabbed them tight around their necks.

The siblings thrashed and slapped helplessly at the long, clasping fingers that held their throats tight. They gasped and gaped as they tried to breathe but could only flounder like perch on the end of a long line, dragged out of the water. The Shadow Wraith reeled them in. "Humans are just so predictable," it mused, its dark eyes glistening in the half-light of the woodland, the water from the pool reflecting in the inky, soulless blackness. "You really think you could evade me by hiding in this filth? If your scent suddenly disappears then, where else would you be? I just had to wait here until you emerged from your pathetic little hidey-hole."

It swung its arms around and threw them onto the forest floor. Bobby felt shards of broken wood and treacherous twigs dig into his skin through his ripped clothes as he fell down heavily, winded. He pulled himself onto all fours and crawled over to his sister. "Katy," he barely managed through his bruised throat. "Katy?"

She nodded back. She was shaken but relatively unharmed.

"So touching," the Wraith sighed. "But now, to business. Tell me who organised the attack on the chapel."

"It was nothing to do with us!" Bobby protested. "We were just passing and got caught up in it."

The Wraith raised a disbelieving eyebrow in a mockery of human emotion. "Really? You just got caught up in the affair and happened to end up on top of a scaffold? Or was that another boy who looked just like you?" He slapped his forehead in mock anguish. "Don't tell me I've been chasing the wrong pair of meddling brats!" His face turned into a vicious scowl and he whipped his left hand out. It shot towards Katy who was still prone on the floor. His hand parted at the end and forked around her neck. The small girl screamed out in shock but even then she wouldn't give up, hitting and smacking the arm with all the strength she had in her small, fatigued body.

The Wraith smiled. "A feisty little thing, isn't she? Tell me, boy, how much energy do you think she'll have when she has no air?" He grinned as his forked hand contracted around Katy's neck. Her eyes started to bulge and her fingers desperately scrabbled at the deformed hand.

Bobby made to lunge towards her but found himself staring at the business end of a construct lance.

"Don't be stupid. Tell me who was in charge of the attack!" roared the Wraith. "If you don't, she dies.

"Followed by you."

Bobby looked on in paralysed horror as Katy's face seemed to start to turn an awful shade of blue and her movements became weaker and weaker. He couldn't let her die. He couldn't. She was all he had.

There was only one thing he could do to save her.

Bobby opened his mouth to speak.

An anguished scream filled the clearing.

The Wraith was staring at the suddenly

truncated end of his arm. Bobby darted to his sister and wrapped her in his arms, holding her preciously close. He looked in awe at the severed hand of the Wraith that now lay on the forest floor, withering to dust, and the sharp metal disk that lay next to it. His head snapped up at the sound of a loud shout and his brain struggled to comprehend just what it saw occur next.

Someone had burst into the clearing. They were swinging a long, heavy stick that connected with the head of the distracted Shadow Wraith, sending it tumbling to the floor. The attacker swung the stick, clubbing it again and again onto the Wraith's head which crumpled under the repeated blows.

But this did not stop the creature. It rolled to one side and, as it rose fluidly to its feet, its mangled features expanded outwards, creating a freshly grown face from which it snarled at its attacker, a man dressed in filthy rags.

A man whom Bobby and Katy recognised.

Cutter.

The monster opened its mouth and

Bobby watched in horror as its jaw dropped far lower than was possible for any creature. An incredibly long prehensile tongue snaked out of the wet, drooling maw and whipped towards Cutter's staff. It circled around the stick and the Wraith yanked back with its powerful neck, forcing the old man to surrender a few paces. Cutter, however, continued to move with the momentum of the attack and dived onto the ground, rolling across the forest floor. This caused the tongue of the beast to lurch sideways, yanking its head round at a completely unnatural angle as Cutter lunged to his feet behind the monster whose head was now facing completely backwards. With a skilful flick of his wrist, the old man snatched his stick out of the grip of the momentarily confused creature as it turned its body around to face the same direction as its head. He then proceeded to advance on the Wraith, dodging from side to side, repeatedly striking its head from first one side, then the other.

The monster raised its damaged arm to protect itself and finally crumpled under the continuous, unrelenting blows.

Within moments, the grizzled old-timer was standing over the vanquished foe, his staff raised and aimed in deadly fashion at the creature's forehead.

"Leave the children be," the children's saviour growled at the fallen Wraith. "They are nothing to you."

The Wraith winced as it flexed its left arm, miraculously sprouting a new hand from the severed clay. Its face glowered ominously like a wild dog that had been soundly kicked with a heavy boot. It was desperate to retaliate but knew that it was beaten. It opened its mouth to speak but Cutter threatened once more with the stick. "No more words; not from you. Just leave."

So the Shadow Wraith did as it was told. It rose elegantly to its feet as if it had risen from a summertime picnic in the woods, casually brushed the leaves and twigs from its clothes then turned and simply walked away into the dense undergrowth.

Cutter turned to the two children. "What on earth have you two gotten yourselves into this time?"

Chapter Six

Smoke rose from a campfire that Cutter had built in a small secluded clearing. They had moved, on his insistence, to another part of the forest. Also on his insistence, Katy and Bobby had taken a bath and had washed their foul-smelling clothes in a clean pool. They were now sat swathed in blankets as their clothes, hung between two trees, were drying next to the warm fire. Suspended above the same fire, a pot bubbled and spat. The delicious aroma emanating from a rabbit stew almost masked the less than pleasant odour of the steam that rose from their clothing.

Cutter poked inquisitively at the contents of the pot, gave a satisfied grunt, and removed it from its hook. He divided the stew between two wooden plates he had produced from his pack and handed it to the children.

"Eat," his gruff voice commanded them. "I don't want you wasting away before your clothes have dried." He then eased himself down onto the forest floor, sat against an old tree and proceeded to fill and light up his long pipe. The fragrant smell of his homemade smoking material drifted up into the air of the clearing and combined with that of the stew.

Katy and Bobby exchanged concerned glances before tucking into the delicious meal. The old man had hardly said two words since he had rescued them from the Shadow Wraith. He had just told them to follow him, which they had gratefully done, then had instructed them to clean themselves up as he wandered off into the undergrowth before returning in a short while with a rabbit that looked like it had been caught with a spear.

Not once had he enquired as to how they had come to be captive of the clay monster.

"It is important that your bellies are full before you explain how you have been so stupid," Cutter said as if reading their minds, speaking around his pipe. "A content body is more likely to be truthful. It has no need to lie." He blew a smoke ring up into the air.

"Are you not going to eat?" Katy asked as she paused her ravenous consumption. "There is plenty here. I don't mind sharing."

The old man looked across at the small girl and Bobby saw a distinct amount of affection touch his face. "It's okay, little one. I am not hungry. You eat it all up. It'll help you grow... as long as you don't do anything stupid like, say, annoy a Shadow Wraith."

Katy and Bobby smiled. They finished their meals in contented silence.

After the meal, their clothes had dried sufficiently in order to be worn, so they dressed themselves and Bobby washed up the pot and plates in the small pond where they had bathed. As he did, Katy sat herself down next to Cutter and stared intently at his pipe.

The old man raised an eyebrow at her in question.

"I like the smell of your pipe."

"So do I. That's why I smoke it."

"What is it you burn in there?"

"A mixture of herbs and tree bark." He looked down at the girl. "Want to try it?"

"Am I allowed?"

Cutter shrugged. "Who's stopping you?"

"No one."

"Then why do you ask if you are allowed?"

She paused. "Because there are certain things we shouldn't do."

The old man held her eyes for a moment then nodded. "It would be wise to remember that, young one."

Bobby walked over and joined them under the tree. "Our father wasn't a fan of smoking," he said.

"That's not what she was talking about." Cutter turned to Katy. "You had no choice, child. Teller..." He shook his head. "He was sick, like a mad dog. He needed putting down or he would have killed you both.

"He was like his father. Some things

run in the family. Madness is one of them."

He held the two children with a steady gaze.

"Honour is another."

Bobby let the words sink in. "You knew our father."

Cutter nodded, his face suddenly sad, tired.

"How?" Bobby asked. "I don't remember meeting you before the other day," he said, referring to their encounter on the road from Irlingbury to Orchester as they had journeyed to take the Eternal Talisman to Jason.

The old man took a thoughtful draw on his long pipe. Bobby could tell that he was carefully choosing the correct words. He had seen his father do the same whenever an awkward customer had made a complaint about something that they thought was wrong with an item that Howard had fashioned for them. Once, there had been a woman who had kept goats. She had ordered a chair upon which she could sit whilst milking her animals. His father had fashioned her a plain, three-legged stool but

the woman had complained that it was bor-
ing and not to her liking. She had said that
she wanted something fancier, something
more pleasing to the eye. Howard had
asked her what she had in mind. She said
that, for starters, she wanted four legs, not
three. She also wanted a back to the stool.
Not just a plain back, either. It had to be in-
tricately carved with birds and ivy. Howard
had held the woman carefully in his gaze before finally asking, "Your goats, do they
clean up after themselves?" The woman
had looked perplexed but had shaken her
head. "The stool you are asking for will not
last a month. Three legs are better than four
because they help to spread the weight of
the person milking the animal. This is important because the ground upon which it
will sit will be soft from the waste and the
trampling of the animal. You do not want the
seat to sink into the ground as you are milking. Also, it needs to be backless or it will be
unbalanced. Animals can be flighty, yes?
They can decide to kick or wriggle, causing
the person milking them to need to readjust
themselves at a moment's notice. If you

have an ornate back to the chair, it will topple over when you suddenly shift your weight. The carving in the wood will either become encrusted with filth or will break, making the furniture impractical and unsightly.

"Sometimes the simpler tool is the most effective."

"I was younger," Cutter explained. "I was a different person back then."

Bobby opened his mouth to ask more, but the old man held up a gnarled hand. "Later. Right now, I'd rather know about how you ended up in the state in which I found you."

So the children explained. They told him everything, about the Eternal Talisman, the Virtuous Man, the plan to destroy the constructs. And, as they spoke, Cutter just sat and smoked on his pipe, his eyes carefully studying the wispy patterns of the aromatic vapours that drifted up into the woodland air.

When they had finished, he studied the bowl of his pipe, tapped out the burnt ash and packed in new ingredients from a leather pouch that he magicked from the depths of his ragged clothes. Taking a steel, he struck a spark into the bowl and the mixture sprung to life. After a few long drags he was satisfied with the result and turned to look at the children.

"What an absolute load of nonsense."

Bobby and Katy exchanged confused looks.

"I assure you it's the truth," Bobby began to protest.

Cutter held up a hand. "Of that I have no doubt, Bobby. You, like your father, are as honest a person as I have ever met. What I mean is..." He shook his head. "A piece of wood and a knife to destroy Kanor? Corralling constructs into an old church and setting fire to them?" He shook his head once more and tutted disconsolately. "Absolute nonsense! I have garnered more sense from a mud-covered swine!" He made to smoke more from his pipe and paused. "This man, Jason. He claims to be the Man of Virtue?"

Bobby and Katy nodded.

"Yet he left all of you to face down those

creatures on your own? Where was he when the fighting began?" He made a disgruntled noise of disgust. "No. He is either a fraud or a fool. When the Virtuous Man comes, he will lead his army from the midst of the battle, not cower at the back like a startled dormouse."

"But what of the Eternal Talisman and the Eternal Dagger?"

"What of them?"

"They are supposed to help him overcome Kanor? How can he not be the Man of Virtue if they have found their way to him?"

Cutter sighed. "If you give a hound a knife, does that make it a swordsman? If you give a rabbit feathers, can it fly? It is nonsense. I don't know what these things are or how they made their way to him, but they are not the things that scare the Black Dragon."

"Does anything scare him?" Katy asked.

Cutter nodded. "Child, everyone is scared of something."

Chapter Seven

After their meal, Cutter suggested that they lie down and get some rest. "You have had a very busy day," he said. "Now is not the time for questions or discussion. Now is the time for recuperation."

"But I'm not sleepy," Katy protested as she stretched her arms and gave a huge yawn.

"I think your body says otherwise," Cutter smiled. "You two curl up here, close your eyes and rest. I will watch over you." The old man turned, rummaged in his pack and produced a small, hand-fashioned recorder. He placed it to his lips and began to play a light, lilting tune.

So it was that, to the relaxing tune of Cutter's lullaby, the children curled up on the soft ground next to the warm fire. Within minutes, they were asleep.

And, as Bobby slept, he dreamed.

His dreams were far from peaceful.

A cruel wind whipped around him as he stood on a high hill overlooking a deep valley. Down below, two armies were fighting. One he recognised immediately. Constructs, hundreds of them marched relentlessly forwards, their arms shaped as lances and scythes. Riding with them were Shadow Wraiths, their cruel faces hungry for battle. Facing off against them were an army of creatures the likes of which he had never before encountered. They were humanoid in shape, two arms, two legs and a head, but they possessed wings. Clad entirely in white, their eyes blazed with fire as they charged towards the creatures of clay. And there, in their midst, was a figure dressed entirely in black. Bobby frowned as he tried to make out the person's face, but it was shrouded by a hood and a material that looked like a thick black gauze swathed its visage.

This unknown warrior was amazing! It

darted between the winged beings and shot into the army of constructs. It possessed a long whip which it cracked left and right, plunging its sharp silver tip through one construct then another, causing them to pause or stumble. Then he would vault and somersault and flicking his weapon out, wrapped it around their heads and pulled tight, making them part into two. The constructs, not yet dead, would stumble and try to pull themselves upright, but then the winged creatures were upon them.

The result was devastating.

From their hands, a green mist emanated. Every construct that the ethereal vapour touched withered and died. It was instant death to the creatures of Kanor.

Yet still the mindless beasts came, onward and onward. But the result was inevitable and at the end of the battle every member of Kanor's army was destroyed. A cheer rose up from the winged beings as they saluted their masked champion.

Bobby wanted to join in. He opened his mouth to praise the warrior, but a dread chill ran down his spine and he was aware that he was no longer alone on the hilltop. His stomach churning, he turned to see a man standing in a dark cowl. He was glowering out across the battlefield, his dark eyes, full of hatred, focussing on the hero of the hour.

He moved his lips and Bobby heard his low voice hiss a single word:

"Claw..."

Bobby woke with a start, his heart pounding against his rib cage. It was dark, early evening and the fire had started to burn low. Katy was still asleep and Cutter was nowhere to be seen.

But that doesn't mean he isn't nearby. Bobby told himself. He knew that the strange old man would be watching. He seemed to be some sort of enigmatic guardian spirit who appeared when necessary.

But who exactly was he?

The more he told them, the more questions it raised about him.

Bobby shook his head. Perhaps one day they would be answered. Right now, it was getting dark and they needed to find shelter. He gently rocked his sister's shoulder. "Katy. Wake up. We need to get going."

Having nowhere else to go, they decided to head back to Orchester. They could stay there the night and then, the following day, head back to Irlingbury, to normality.

"It'll be nice to go home," Bobby said as they approached the edge of the small village. "We can put all this behind us and go back to our lives."

Katy was curiously silent.

"What's up?" he asked.

She just shrugged.

Bobby sighed. More questions. Well, they could just wait. Right now they needed somewhere safe to shelter. "I think we're best finding an empty house on the outskirts. I don't really want to cross paths with Jason right now," he said.

"And why might that be?" came a familiar voice from behind them.

Bobby and Katy turned to the sound of the voice and gasped at the sight of Jason standing behind them with a group of villagers. The children didn't take the time to consider whether this was a good thing or not. Without a word, the two siblings did what they seemed to do best.

They ran.

Is this to be our lot in life now? Bobby wondered to himself as he and Katy sped down first one cluttered alley then another, leaping over discarded piles of refuse and dodging around broken and discarded household items. It certainly seemed to be that way as the angry shouts of pursuing villagers followed them through the unfamiliar passageways.

Had this been Irlingbury, he and Katy would have used familiar routes to escape those who wanted back their fruit that the street kids had stolen. They knew their home town like the backs of their hands, every nook and cranny: every dead end to avoid and every abandoned house in which to lay low.

Orchester, however, was a completely different story.

Time and time again they skidded around a blind corner to be presented with yet another cul-de-sac or a means of escape that was blocked, causing them to double back and seek another route. Consequently, with every wrong turn, any lead on their pursuers that their youth and swift feet had provided was gradually whittled away, until it felt like the baying mob were literally breathing down their necks.

But they knew that they had to keep running. Jason's voice had sounded far from friendly. He did not seem at all delighted to see them returned safe and sound from their doomed mission. In fact, he sounded just as dangerous as the Shadow Wraith that they had previously encountered.

"Bobby, it's another dead end!" Katy wailed as they found themselves once more facing a sheer wall at the end of a blind alley. "Do these people have no idea how to plan a village?"

The sound of running and shouting was now closer than ever. Bobby whipped his head from side to side and caught sight of a small door in a darkened corner of the back street. "Katy! Here!" He ran over to the door, his sister right behind him, wrapped his hands around the handle and pushed.

Nothing. No movement.

He pushed again, leaning forwards with all his weight.

Still nothing.

Anger and frustration consumed the boy as he physically threw himself at the door. They had to escape, they had to. Again he launched himself at the small door and still it remained resolutely shut. Tears of frustration welled up in his eyes as saw all the hardship they had suffered over the last few days personified in this rectangle of faded wood and he screamed at the top of his voice as he charged forwards, colliding with the locked door. But his onslaught did not stop there. He pounded against it with his fists, screaming inarticulately with previously suppressed rage into the cold night air.

He only stopped when the firm hand of a villager fell on his shoulder.

Bobby sank to his knees, defeated.

Bobby and Katy had barely any energy left and could only put up the vaguest of struggles as they were dragged into the village square.

Jason was stood there with more angry-looking villagers. Set up behind them were two stout poles which had wood piled up around their bases.

This did not look good.

"Citizens of Orchester," Jason called out those who stood around them. "You know me. You know what I stand for, how I bring society hope. We need to rise up and overthrow that vile dragon who has destroyed our world. You know that I will lead you in this.

"Yet there are those," he pointed at Bobby and Katy, "who would see us fail."

The villagers shouted and hurled abuse at the two children. Jason motioned towards the two poles and they were dragged over and tied roughly to the wood.

"You have all heard of your kindred's valiant attempt to destroy a contingent of constructs. They came so close to success. They had ensnared them and had set fire to them. But they were betrayed by these two incomers."

"That's a lie!" Bobby shouted. "Your plan was flawed. It failed. We almost died."

"You dare to accuse me of falsehood?" Jason screamed back at him. "You know who I am. I am the Man of Virtue. I have the Eternal Talisman and the Eternal Dagger. I am tasked with destroying Kanor himself. How dare you try to pin blame on me?" He paused and composed himself, running a hand through his glossy black hair. "No, these *supposed* children sabotaged my efforts and allowed the constructs to slaughter your friends and family. I say we test them. Show them for what they really are.

"Servants of Kanor."

It was as a villager stepped forwards with a burning torch that Bobby realised what the wood around their feet was for. "No! No! You can't be serious! We're human!"

"You are heartless beasts of clay. You are soulless denizens of Kanor and you must be destroyed." He nodded to the villager and the woman began to lower the torch.

There was a cracking noise and Bobby

watched a whip lash itself around the woman's wrist, yanking it backwards, causing the torch to fall harmlessly to the floor. The rest happened faster than he could possibly perceive.

A figure strode into the midst of the villagers who were yelling, shouting and taking up arms. He was clad from head to toe in black and as they charged him, he leapt gracefully up into the night air. As he descended, his feet kicked out causing those close to him to fall backwards and his silver-tipped whip swung around in a wide circle, making others stagger backwards.

Bobby had just caught sight of Jason darting out of the village square when he heard a woman's voice behind him. "Hold still," it said as his bonds fell free. "Now hold your breath."

He felt a strong pair of arms encircle his middle and suddenly the world flashed past him in a total blur. He gasped for air and blinked his eyes as he found himself being settled down at the edge of what looked like a field, but he was so startled, it could have been the moon for all he knew. The woman let go of him and pulled back, a lopsided grin on her face. By the light of the rising moon, Bobby saw a pair of sparkling green eyes and a shock of short red hair. He saw movement to his left and a blur transformed into a blonde-haired woman coming to a stop with Katy in her arms.

There was another flicker of movement as a third shadow transformed into the man with the whip. He pulled back his hood, revealing a concerned face. "Are they okay?" he asked the redhead.

"Absolutely fine."

The man nodded. "Hello Bobby," he said. "My name is Claw."

Bobby Normal will return in
Bobby Normal and the Children of Cain.

A.S.Chambers

Author's Notes

So, welcome to the end of Bobby's second outing. I hope it has answered some questions for you but left you with a few more teasers to keep your curiosity piqued and hungry for more.

At the time of writing, there are exactly six days until *Bobby Normal and the Eternal Talisman*, the first book in this series, is due to be published. In short, for once in my writing career, I am actually ahead of myself. This is a curious and most agreeable situation to find myself in. Normally, when writing the Sam Spallucci books, I find myself starting off with great gusto but then, because of the size and growing complexity of the *Spallucciverse*, I end up playing catch up towards the end of the project and only just sketching out the next book as I publish the current one. Because of the size and style of the Bobby Normal books, they now seem to be emerging thick and fast. This one took just two months to write the first draft!

So, what lies ahead for the characters in the book?

Well, as for Jason, if you've read my short story *The Virtuous Man* in my 2020 anthology *Hide Not Thou Thy Face*, then you will already know that his confrontation with Kanor does not go quite according to plan.

Cutter is developing really nicely and I know from my beta readers of *BNET* that he is going to be a firm fan favourite, especially as he lets slip more of his back story and his past relationship with the Normal family.

The nameless Shadow Wraith was great fun to write. The constructs are my (as well as Kanor's) soulless, clay-based, relentlessly murderous babies. I love how a creature with no features can actually possess personality and I wanted to take that further. So, creating a more developed version gave me a chance to play with that.

Watch this space for more of his kind, along with the third denizens of the Divergent Lands, the as yet unmet Fallen.

So, as the next book in the series is entitled *Bobby Normal and the Children of Cain*, it should be rather apparent who the saviours of our heroes are, whisking them away from a fiery death in Orchester. The more eagle-eyed constant readers of my books should easily be able to identify the blonde and the redhead. And then there is Claw… Serious spoilers that way lie. He has been seen before in dreams in Sam's books, but I don't recall him ever having been named. Claw is obviously his vampire name, but what might he have previously been called and have you already come across him? I would appreciate your thoughts on that one. Who knows, there may be a very obvious clue in the next Bobby Normal outing.

Then there is Bobby and his kid sister Katy. Just trust me when I say that I have far more dangerous adventures ahead for them as they get drawn deeper and deeper into a shadowy world where the forces of light are desperately trying to scrabble their way back to the fore and overthrow the black dragon of Kanor in an attempt to bring an end to the Divergent Lands.

ASC June 2021.

ABOUT THE AUTHOR

A.S.Chambers resides in Lancaster, England. He lives a fairly simple life measuring the growing rates of radishes and occasionally puts pen to paper to stop the voices in his head from constantly berating him.

He is quite happy for, and in fact would encourage, you to follow him on Facebook, Instagram and Twitter.

There is also a nice, shiny website:
www.aschambers.co.uk